Imagine Me A Pirate!

Mark Marshall

I'm lively, fearless and clever,
And as brave as a dog can be!
Always looking for adventure –
So come on a journey with me . . .

Imagine I'm a pirate, Upon the open seas.

Sailing in my shipshape boat, to anywhere I please.

Imagine I'm an astronaut
Blasting into space!

I'd wave to my friends on the Earth below,
And disappear without a trace!

I'd wear a special spacedog's suit
with a helmet for my face.
I could leave my paw prints on the moon,
And offer aliens a race!

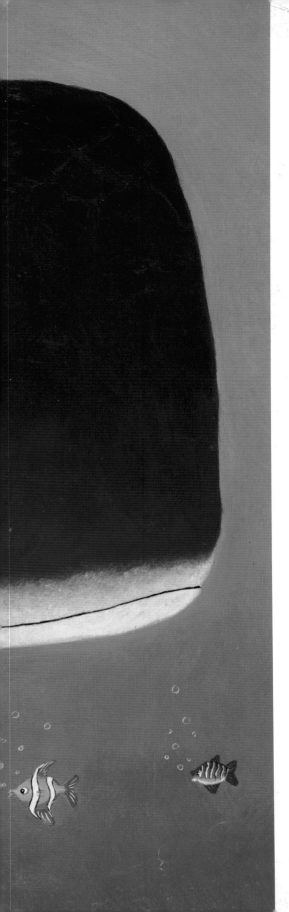

He could squirt me with his water-spout
And catch me with his tail.

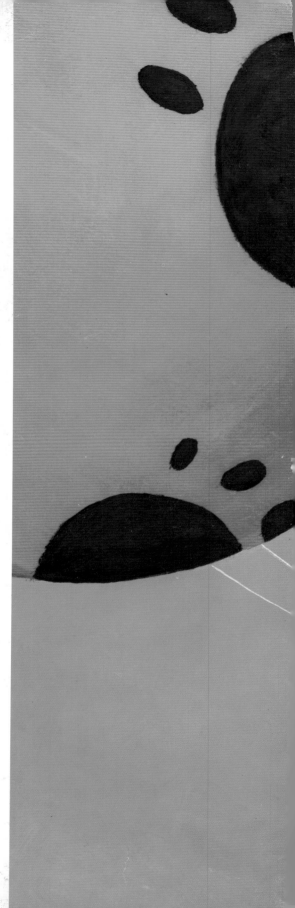

Imagine I'm the pilot
Of my own hot air balloon.
I'd spot a stripy zebra
Or catch sight of a baboon!

Imagine I'm an explorer,
Trekking to the cold North Pole

I might just find an igloo
Made from bricks of ice
And I could join the bear in there –
Now wouldn't that be nice!

I love to dream my doggy dreams –
They challenge and inspire!
But the best place on earth for me right now . . .

Is curled up and warm
by the fire.